# Antics

## THE POTTY PENGUIN

For Alfie, as brave and hopeful as Pepper – LC

For Isabelle – PA

STRIPES PUBLISHING
An imprint of Magi Publications
1 The Coda Centre, 189 Munster Road,
London SW6 6AW

A paperback original
First published in Great Britain in 2010

Text copyright © Lucy Courtenay, 2010
Illustrations copyright © Phil Alderson, 2010

ISBN: 978-1-84715-146-9

Printed and bound in the UK.

10 9 8 7 6 5 4 3 2 1

# Animal Antics

## THE POTTY PENGUIN

### LUCY COURTENAY

Illustrated by Phil Alderson

**stripes**

# Animals!

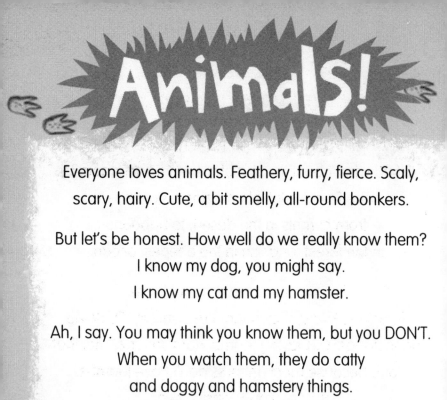

Everyone loves animals. Feathery, furry, fierce. Scaly, scary, hairy. Cute, a bit smelly, all-round bonkers.

But let's be honest. How well do we really know them?
I know my dog, you might say.
I know my cat and my hamster.

Ah, I say. You may think you know them, but you DON'T.
When you watch them, they do catty
and doggy and hamstery things.
But what about when you're not watching?
Who knows what they do when you're snoozing
in your beds or when you're at school?

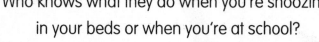

And what about the rest of the animal kingdom?
The world is full of amazing creatures –
from camels in the desert, to baboons
in the forest, and fish in the deepest ocean.

We know even less about them.
For all we know, they might like dancing. Or doing
handstands. Or playing thumb wars. Actually, not that
one because most animals don't have thumbs.
But you know what I mean.

Maybe we don't know animals as well as we think.
Take **PENGUINS,** for instance…

# Chapter One

Pepper was a small Emperor penguin with a Big Secret.

Pepper's secret was so big that she hadn't told anyone about it. Not her dad. Not her mum. Not even her best friend Petal. Pepper hugged her Big Secret close to her chest, where it was safe and no one could laugh at it.

Pepper wanted to fly.

# Animal Antics

Pepper had always loved watching the birds in the Antarctic sky. She had gasped at their twists and turns. She had cheered as they flew out of reach of the hungry seals that tried to catch them as they bobbed on the sea. And she had wished with all her little penguin heart that she could be up there too, flying and twisting, turning and floating like a cloud.

It was true that penguins didn't normally fly. But Pepper had a hopeful nature. She KNEW that one day she would do it. She just had to *practise*.

# Animal Antics

Practising is hard to do when you don't want anyone to know what you're practising for. As soon as she lost her soft grey down and grew some proper feathers, Pepper started sneaking off behind rocks and icebergs. She did lots of flapping exercises with her stubby flippers. She jumped and stretched out her neck on take-off, the way she'd seen other birds do. She'd been practising for several months now, and so far no one had seen her. But in a colony of penguins, keeping secrets was almost impossible.

"Where *have* you been, Pepper?" her dad said one day when Pepper returned to the shore of the Southern Ocean, breathless and covered in snow.

"Just … exploring," said Pepper. A large lump of ice fell off her beak.

Her dad frowned. "You look like you fell in a snowdrift."

"I did," said Pepper.

"I don't understand this urge to explore, Pepper," her dad said. "All you'll find out there is snow and ice. And maybe a rock or two. And snow and ice. And seals who will eat you as soon as look at you. And did I mention the snow and ice? The snow and ice are the worst."

"Yes, Dad," said Pepper.

"You have to watch your step," her father said.

Pepper *had* watched her step. She'd watched it very carefully as she jumped off the rock and flapped like crazy. It hadn't helped.

"I'll watch it better in future," she said.

"Forget about exploring," her dad advised. "Let me see you practise your swimming instead. You'll find it easier now you've got a full set of feathers."

# Animal Antics

Pepper wanted to get back to her flying practice. She felt she'd been really close to flying on her last jump, before the snowdrift got in the way. But with her dad watching, she had no choice but to jump into the sea.

Pepper enjoyed swimming. She supposed it was a bit like flying, the way she could zoom along with her flippers. She closed her eyes and imagined she was in the air.

Swimming with your eyes closed is a bad idea. As Pepper rose to the surface, she crashed into another penguin.

"Sorry," she gasped. She opened her eyes to see a small penguin with merry eyes laughing at her. "Ooh, it's you, Petal!" she said, pleased to see her best friend.

"Pepper, you twit," said Petal with a grin. "What are you doing, swimming around with your eyes closed?"

# Animal Antics

Pepper had known Petal her entire life. Their dads had stood next to each other while Pepper and Petal were still eggs, keeping them warm and away from the ice by balancing them on their feet and nestling their feathers over the top. Pepper and Petal had hatched on the same day. So the first thing Pepper saw, apart from her dad's feathery bottom, was Petal peeping out from underneath her own father's tummy.

But even though Petal was her best friend, Pepper wasn't ready to tell her about the flying yet. It was too precious.

"The salty water stings my eyes," she fibbed.

"That's weird," said Petal. "My eyes are fine. Where have you been anyway, Pepper? I haven't seen you all day. There's a new toboggan run I want to show you."

Pepper was trying to think of something to

tell Petal when a long ripply black shadow passed across the blue water.

"A seal!" Pepper gasped in fright.

As Pepper's dad often reminded her, seals ate penguins. Especially young ones who weren't as wise or as fast as adults. There was a scramble as everyone rushed for the shore. Chubby penguin bodies sprang out of the water and skidded to safety, including Pepper and Petal.

The shadow now passed from the water on to the shore, making a clear blue outline against the white ice. Pepper looked up.

High in the sky was a huge bird. Its snow-white body hung lazily in the air. Its long yellow beak gleamed like sunshine. Its great black and white wings stretched out on either side.

"Phew," said Petal. "It wasn't a seal. It was just a silly albatross."

# Animal Antics

Pepper stared in awe at the albatross. She'd never seen one before. She didn't think there was anything silly about it at all. Unable to help herself, she stretched out her flippers and thrust out her neck. In her mind, she was up there with the albatross, soaring through the sky.

Pepper's dream only lasted as long as her balance. Her body tipped forward and she planted her beak deep into the ice.

"Pepper! What happened?" said Petal. "Are you OK?"

Pepper had a feeling she looked stupid. She flapped her flippers, but her beak was stuck fast.

"Fne," she mumbled, as breezily as she could. "Dnt wrry abt me, Ptl. M fne."

# Chapter Two

With a lot of tugging, Pepper finally pulled her beak out of the ice. Petal tried to help, but when you've only got flippers there's not a lot you can do to pull your friends back on to their feet.

With so many penguins in the colony, there was only the tiniest chance that no one had seen Pepper fall over. But when you are a hopeful sort of penguin, a tiny chance is better

than no chance at all. Pepper crossed her
flippers and checked.

At least twenty penguins were roaring with
laughter and pointing their flippers at her.
Pepper's heart sank. Penguins were gossips.
Her little accident would be all over the colony
in no time at all.

The albatross was still in the sky, hanging
there like a serene black and white cloud.
Watching it made Pepper feel better. How did
it *do* that? Stay so still? It wasn't even flapping
its wings.

The albatross bent one wing very gently.
It moved off, flying sideways and out of sight.
It made flying look as easy as tobogganing.

Pepper spoke without thinking. "I'm going
to do that one day," she said.

Petal followed Pepper's gaze. "You're
going to *fly*?" she gasped.

# Animal Antics

Pepper felt flustered. She hadn't meant to say anything.

"You just said you're going to fly!" repeated Petal.

"Yes," Pepper said in a quiet voice. "I am."

"That has to be your craziest idea ever, Pepper," Petal giggled. "Penguins can't fly! I mean, we can kind of fly when we swim and when we toboggan, but proper flying? Like an albatross? No way!"

Pepper felt hurt. She lifted her chin. "Who says penguins can't fly?" she replied.

"Have you ever seen a flying penguin?" Petal asked.

"Just because I haven't seen one, it doesn't mean penguins can't do it," Pepper said.

"You're mad, Pepper," Petal laughed.

Normally, Pepper would have laughed back and changed the subject. But flying was her most precious dream, and she didn't like Petal's tone of voice. "Thanks for nothing," she said crossly. "I suppose you'll tell everyone now and they'll laugh at me even more."

Petal's eyes widened. "I promise I won't tell anyone," she said. "But Pepper – you really won't ever be able to fly. Penguins just can't."

But Pepper was already waddling away. She wasn't used to feeling sad, and she didn't want Petal to see the tears that had started rushing down her cheeks.

Snow began to fall in heavy white sheets. Pepper headed for her best place: a rock overlooking the ocean. She liked it there because if she stood close to the edge and stretched out her neck, she could pretend she was flying over the sea. She hoped it would make her feel better, and make the strange knotted feeling in her stomach go away.

# Animal Antics

To her dismay, Pom was waiting for her.

Pom was large and lazy. He was older than Pepper, but he hadn't learned how to fish yet. He was Pepper's least favourite penguin in the colony. Since there were about fifty thousand penguins to choose from, this was pretty bad. He was also, unfortunately, Pepper's cousin.

"I can't believe you got your beak stuck in the ice!" Pom hooted.

"Oh, go and regurgitate a fish, Pom," Pepper muttered.

Pom did a little dance, flapping his wings and pretending to be Pepper. "Mmph, mmph, mmph!" he mumbled through his closed beak. "Ha ha! Wish I'd seen it!"

Pepper tried to pretend she hadn't been heading for the rock overlooking the ocean at all. She waddled past Pom with her chin held high and headed for one of her favourite toboggan runs instead. But she couldn't enjoy the feeling of the smooth, slippery ice whizzing away under her tummy. She was still feeling upset about Petal. How could her best friend have laughed at her like that? Pepper had been right to keep her Big Secret a secret.

# Animal Antics

The toboggan run brought Pepper out near her favourite fishing ground, Silver Cove. The fish were so thick in the cove that it was nearly impossible *not* to catch one. There were no other penguins there today, which suited Pepper's strange, unhappy mood.

With three fish safely in her tummy and a comfy spot on an ice floe, it wasn't long before Pepper started feeling positive again. She stretched out her flippers and studied them. They were more or less the same shape as the albatross's wings. Just a bit smaller. And a bit less feathery. But apart from the size and feathers, what exactly was the difference? Why couldn't penguins fly? Had anyone ever tried?

# Chapter Three

Pepper stood up. Her ice floe was thick, and the water was some way down. If she took a run-up, she might be able to fly a little way before landing in the sea.

Feeling excited now, Pepper backed up so her heels were off the back of the floe. She held her flippers out as she'd seen the albatross do with its wings. Then she started running.

# Animal Antics

The ice floe wasn't very big, but Pepper's legs were short and the run-up took longer than she expected. By the time she reached the edge, she was completely out of breath. Puffing and snorting like a walrus, she threw all her remaining energy into a massive leap over the edge.

Pointing her beak at the sky, Pepper tried to think about albatrosses and clouds and dancing snowflakes. Anything to make herself a bit lighter. But almost at once, she was falling.

She stopped trying to glide and thrummed her flippers madly, her feet flailing through the air. The water was getting closer. If she couldn't turn round, she would do an extremely painful bottom flop.

She looked down at the fast-approaching water. And suddenly she realized why there were no penguins fishing there today.

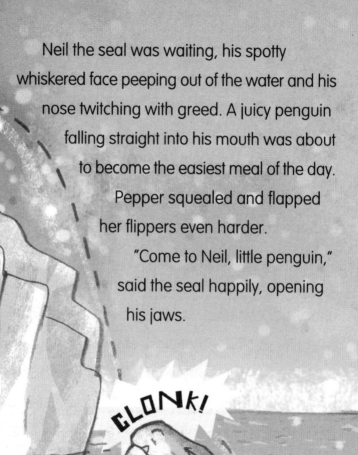

Neil the seal was waiting, his spotty whiskered face peeping out of the water and his nose twitching with greed. A juicy penguin falling straight into his mouth was about to become the easiest meal of the day. Pepper squealed and flapped her flippers even harder.

"Come to Neil, little penguin," said the seal happily, opening his jaws.

CLONK!

# Animal Antics

Pepper landed squarely on Neil's nose, slamming his jaws shut.

"MMPH!" Neil said in surprise.

Before the seal could open his mouth again, Pepper slid down his back and started swimming for her life. Her flippers had never worked so hard as she powered through the water towards the shore.

*Oh please,* she prayed. *Oh please, please, please…*

# Animal Antics

Neil turned, chasing Pepper with his mouth open wider than ever. Pepper put on a fresh burst of speed. She zigzagged from side to side as she tried to avoid the seal's teeth. With a mighty effort she flung herself ashore, landing on her tummy so hard that she winded herself.

"Oh poo," said the great seal crossly.

Neil was happy chasing penguins when he was ashore and happy chasing penguins when he was in the water. But heaving his big blubbery body from one to the other wasn't much fun, and he tried to avoid it. He was beaten this time, and he knew it.

So did Pepper. "Poo to you too," she said, from the safety of a high ridge of ice.

Neil blinked his bulbous black eyes at her. "Next time," he said. "For sure, my fat little penguin. Next time, I'll swallow you in one bite."

The big seal swam slowly out of sight, leaving Pepper to get her breath back. Thinking about her narrow escape made her feel faint. If she'd been able to fly, she would never have crashed into Neil. The thought made her more determined than ever to learn how to do it.

She waddled away from the water's edge towards the great carved ice fields inland. She needed to find somewhere *really* high in order to practise properly. Somewhere, she hoped, without seals.

# Animal Antics

Before long, the ice under Pepper's feet began to rise. She started puffing with the effort of walking. After a while, she paused for breath and looked around. The snow had stopped, and she had a good view from where she stood. The shore below was speckled with the thousands of black, white and yellow Emperor penguins of her colony, the blue water of the Southern Ocean stretching away beyond it. A range of jagged white mountains stood in the other direction. Pepper wondered if she should try jumping off a mountain. Then she remembered how much even a snowdrift could hurt if you landed on it wrongly. Maybe she should leave the mountains to the birds who already knew how to fly.

Pepper waddled on. Then she gasped.

She was standing at the edge of a large rock, looking down at a perfect blanket of fresh snow far below. The view would have scared most penguins. But to Pepper, who was brave as well as hopeful, it was perfect.

She stuck her beak up into the air and tested the wind. It was blowing steadily in from the sea. From what she'd seen of the way birds used the wind, this was good news. It meant she would jump with the wind behind her. She was *bound* to fly this time.

Before she could think too hard about what she was about to do, Pepper took a deep breath and spread her flippers.

"Penguins for ever!" she shouted.

And she jumped.

LEAP!

## Chapter Four

The wind whistled past Pepper's ears as she flapped. She was gathering speed … but not in a good way.

*Plenty of time to get it right,* Pepper told herself. *The snow is still a long way down.*

She turned her flippers very slightly, hoping to get some lift. Nothing. She tipped her body forward more and lifted her feet behind her.

Still nothing. She tried stretching out her neck. Nope. Maybe if she just—

But Pepper had run out of sky. She hit the snow headfirst. Luckily for her, it was soft and powdery. She landed in it so deep that only her feet were left waving in the air. Then she toppled sideways, bringing half the snowdrift with her.

As Pepper lay there gasping for breath, she couldn't help feeling a twinge of concern. Conditions had been perfect, but she still hadn't flown.

What else could she possibly do?

"Ehem," said a voice.

Pepper turned her head. A gigantic bird was standing behind her. Her eyes travelled the length of its great white body. She gazed at the curved yellow beak and the bird's fierce black eyes. One wing was tucked closely into its body.

The other was hanging at a strange angle by the bird's side. It blended almost perfectly with the snow.

"Are you the albatross?" she said in wonder.

The albatross looked confused.

"I mean," Pepper said, "are you the albatross who's been flying over my colony?"

"I have flown over many colonies," said the albatross.

It unfolded the wing that was close to its body and stretched it out. Pepper's eyes grew round. The bird's wing went on and on and on. It was three times the length of Pepper herself.

"You are!" she squealed, recognizing the albatross's speckled black wing tip. "You're *that* albatross! What are you doing on the ground? I didn't think albatrosses ever landed anywhere except the sea!"

"They don't," said the albatross. He had a deep, rather serious voice. "I had an accident."

"Poor you!" Pepper said happily.

"There's no need to look so pleased about it," the albatross said. "My wing hurts quite a lot. I think I've sprained it."

He pointed his long beak at the wing that was trailing down.

"Sorry," said Pepper. "It's just – if you hadn't had an accident I wouldn't be talking to you. And I'm so glad to be talking to you. I think you're wonderful!"

"Under normal circumstances, I would agree with you," the albatross said.

"How did you hurt yourself?" Pepper asked.

"I clipped my wing on a cliff," the albatross said. "I've been flying for forty years and I've never clipped my wing on anything." He sounded rather cross with the cliff.

"At least you can fly," Pepper said wistfully. "What's your name?"

"Alvaro," said the albatross. "I'm cold and hungry. And sore. And to make things worse, I can't even move my feet."

Pepper noticed that the albatross's large feet were stuck to a stretch of glittering ice just beside her snowdrift. Trying not to think about

what would have happened if she'd hit the ice and not the snowdrift moments earlier – or indeed if she'd hit the albatross himself – Pepper inspected the problem more closely.

"You've been standing there too long," she said.

# Animal Antics

"I didn't think about moving my feet when I was checking my wing," said the albatross. "Albatrosses rarely think about their feet."

Pepper was thrilled. She was talking to the thing she most admired in the whole world!

"Why don't you sit down for a bit?" she suggested. "Your body heat will melt the ice."

"Sit down?" said Alvaro. "Albatrosses never sit down."

Pepper could see that Alvaro was offended at the thought of sitting down. "Perhaps just this once?" she said.

Alvaro lowered his snowy body over his great webbed feet with a grumble and a groan. Pepper saw him wince as he jarred his injured wing. She sat beside him on the snow and waited. After several minutes, the albatross stood up again. His feet came away from the ice with a squelch.

"Thank you, small penguin," he said, shaking out one leg and then the other.

"Call me Pepper," Pepper beamed.

"Thank you, Pepper," said the albatross.

"No problem, Alvaro," said Pepper.

"I can't hunt with my sprained wing," Alvaro said. "Could you find me some food? I just need a few days' rest and then I'll be off."

"Of course I can," Pepper said, deciding to ignore the fact that the albatross hadn't said please. "But I've got a favour to ask you as well."

# Animal Antics

Alvaro looked down his golden beak at her. "Would this have something to do with your attempt at flying just now?"

Pepper blushed. She hadn't seen Alvaro as she jumped, but Alvaro had clearly seen *her*.

"Yes," she mumbled.

"Penguins don't usually want to fly," said Alvaro. "What makes you different?"

"I suppose I'm not a very usual penguin," Pepper said. Her dreams came out in a rush. "I want to see so many things. I want to know what it's like to have the whole sky around me, and I want to look at the whole world from up above because it must look totally different, and I want to turn in the wind and feel it rushing over my back. If I fetch food for you for the next couple of days, will you teach me how to fly? Will you? Please, Alvaro? Please?"

# Chapter Five

Alvaro the albatross tried to put Pepper off.
He pointed out that penguins had never flown.
He reminded Pepper that she was made for
moving through the water, not the air. He told
her she would never succeed. Pepper refused
to take no for an answer.

"I know it might not work," she said, "but I
have to try. You're my best chance."

"And if I can't teach you, what then?" said Alvaro.

Pepper bowed her head. "I suppose if I can't learn from an albatross, then I can't learn at all," she said.

"Very well," said Alvaro. "I'll teach you what I know. You must listen carefully and do exactly what I say. Do you promise me that?"

"Yes," said Pepper at once. "I promise."

"Right," said Alvaro. "Our first lesson…"

Pepper spread her stubby flippers eagerly.

"…will take place just as soon as you've fetched me some fish to eat," Alvaro continued.

Disappointed, Pepper lowered her flippers. "I'll be back as soon as I can," she said. "Don't go away!"

She waddled so fast down to Silver Cove that she almost broke into a run. She knew a short cut where the ground slid steeply down to the water's edge. Tobogganing was almost as good as flying, the way the air whistled past her cheeks and flowed over her streamlined body.

She slowed herself down before the great cliff that hung over the bay, and waddled down to the edge of the water.

# Animal Antics

As always, Silver Cove teemed with fish. They twisted around each other like eels in a rockpool, just asking to be caught. Pepper checked for signs of Neil, but the seal was nowhere to be seen.

Petal was swimming in the cove. Seeing her best friend made Pepper feel a bit funny. She wondered what to say. They had never argued before.

"Hi, Pepper!" called Petal, swimming over as Pepper hesitated on the shore. "Are you feeling better? I'm sorry I upset you this morning."

Pepper grinned with relief. "I'm sorry I got cross with you," she said. "It's just…" She stopped, feeling awkward.

"I won't laugh at you ever again," Petal said. "If you want to fly, I'm sure you'll manage it somehow."

# Animal Antics

"Thanks," said Pepper gratefully. "I've started having lessons actually," she added, as Petal jumped out of the water to join her on the shore. "From the albatross we saw!"

Petal looked amazed.

"He's stuck out in the ice fields with an injured wing, and I'm catching some fish for him so he'll teach me," Pepper went on. Now Petal had promised not to laugh, it felt really good talking to her. "But it's a total secret, OK? Promise not to tell?"

"I promise," said Petal. "I'm really happy for you, Pepper."

And the two best friends touched beaks affectionately.

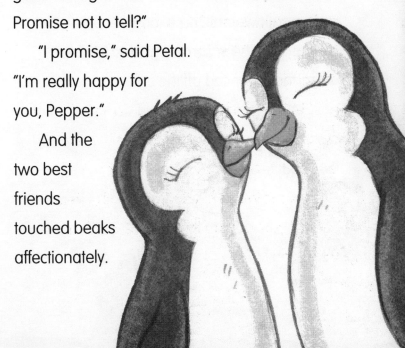

# Animal Antics

With Petal's help, Pepper caught three fish almost at once, which she laid out neatly on the shore. As she bobbed up with a fourth, she saw Petal pointing frantically. Pom was scooping Alvaro's fish into his chubby beak.

"They aren't yours, Pom!" Pepper said in dismay.

"They are now!" Pom tipped his head back and swallowed all three, one after the other. "Yum yum," he said, and gave a loud fishy burp that bounced off the cliff.

# Animal Antics

"You lazy lump!" Petal shouted. "I hope Neil the seal gets you!"

Pom glanced around, then relaxed. "No seals today," he said smugly.

"Neil was here earlier, you know," Pepper yelled at Pom. "I only just got away from him – and you're loads slower than me!"

"All the more reason to let you catch my fish," grinned Pom. He settled down on the edge of the water. "I don't see why I should learn how when I've got a nice little slave to do it for me. Bring me another or I'll peck you when you get out!"

"Pommy!"

Pom's head jerked round. A large female penguin was waddling down to the shore. It was Pom's mother, Pepper's Aunt Primrose.

"Pomsicle!" Aunt Primrose warbled. "PomPom! Time for dindins! I've regurgitated a scrummy yummy fishy-wish for you! Come to Mumsy!"

"Go to Mumsy then, Pomsicle!" Pepper shouted, grinning at Pom's embarrassment. "Go and get your fishy-wish!"

"Leave the real fishing to more mature penguins, why don't you?" Petal added, laughing.

Pom hunched his shoulders and waddled after his mother. In a funny way, Pepper felt a bit sorry for him.

When Pepper had caught four more fish and said goodbye to Petal, she headed back out to the ice fields with her catch. It took less than five seconds for all four fish to disappear down the albatross's throat. Pepper waited, hopping from foot to foot.

# Animal Antics

"Can you teach me now?" she said, unable to contain herself any longer. "Please?"

"If you want to fly," Alvaro began, "the first thing you must do is build up the strength in your, er – wings."

The albatross demonstrated with his healthy wing. He caused such a wind that Pepper almost fell over.

Eagerly, she stood on tiptoe and flapped her flippers the way the albatross had done. Alvaro nodded.

"You must do a hundred of those before each meal every day, Pepper," he said.

"Brilliant!" said Pepper. "I'll definitely do that. What next?"

"That's it for today," said Alvaro.

"That's it?" said Pepper in disappointment.

Alvaro looked severe. "I didn't say it would be quick," he said.

"No," said Pepper sadly. "I suppose you didn't."

"I need to rest now," said the albatross. "Four more fish for breakfast in the morning, please. And look out for seals on your way home. I know how much they like you little penguins."

# Chapter Six

Pepper wasn't sure she liked Alvaro all that much.

He was magnificent, certainly. He was polite most of the time. And he was teaching her about wind currents, aerodynamics and everything else he knew about flying. But he was also bossy and grand. If Pepper didn't catch enough fish, he sent her back to Silver

# Animal Antics

Cove with a flick of his long yellow beak. He made Pepper do a hundred flaps at the start of each lesson. He also talked about himself. A lot.

"Of course," Alvaro said, as Pepper puffed away at her exercises, "you can only imagine the splendour of my life. I am away for months at a time. Years. I have seen things you little penguins can only dream of. Ah, life on the open sea!"

"Eighty-nine," Pepper puffed. "Ninety. Ninety-one…"

"My dear mate Anthea was lucky to get me," Alvaro continued. "She danced like a feather in the wind when we met, so naturally I couldn't resist her. But I had my pick of the lady albatrosses."

"Ninety-four," Pepper went on grimly. "Ninety-five. Ninety-six…"

"We've raised several strong chicks together," Alvaro continued. "Our latest youngster is almost one, I believe. Of course, I'm an excellent parent. Most albatrosses are."

It struck Pepper that if Alvaro was away at sea for months or years at a time, it would be hard to be a parent, and even harder to be a good one. She thought of her dad patiently teaching her how to fish. Her mum was away hunting at the moment, but she was never gone for long. Pepper felt a bit sorry for Alvaro's chicks.

"A hundred," she panted, lowering her aching flippers. "Finished. Can I jump off something now?"

Alvaro nodded at a nearby rock. Pepper hurried to the top and flung herself off with her usual enthusiasm.

"No, no, no," Alvaro tutted, as Pepper plummeted into the snow. "Remember what I told you about catching the wind at precisely the right angle. A hundred more flaps, I think. Now, did I tell you about the time I flew all the way around the world?"

By the third day of Pepper's flying lessons, Alvaro was getting stronger. So were Pepper's flippers. At least, she hoped they were. She was flapping them enough. But no matter what she did, she still ended up with a beak full of ice and Alvaro's despairing sighs ringing in her ears.

After her lesson on the fourth day, Pepper waddled back to the colony, thinking reluctantly that perhaps Petal was right. Perhaps she would never fly.

On the rock that overlooked the ocean,

Pepper found Pom and Aunt Primrose chatting with Pepper's dad. Aunt Primrose was doing most of the talking. She talked even more than Alvaro did.

"Ah, here's Pepper!" said Pepper's dad, interrupting Aunt Primrose with relief. "Where have you been, Pepper? Exploring again, eh?"

"Little Pomwom loves exploring," said Aunt Primrose immediately. "He's such a brave little chick! Always off and about in the sea!"

*Stealing other penguins' fish*, Pepper thought. "That's funny, Aunt Primrose," she said. "I never see little Pomwom in the sea."

Pom glared at her.

"Well, of course my little Pomsicle does swim extremely fast," Aunt Primrose said, stroking her bright yellow ear patches with her flippers. "He outswam Neil the seal the other day, he told me! Can you imagine? So brave!"

Pom now stared at the sky and wouldn't
meet Pepper's eye. *Typical*, Pepper thought.
*Pom doesn't just steal my fish. He steals my
stories too.*

Aunt Primrose hawked up a particularly
stinky bit of fish and fed it to Pom. "I've made
him promise not to swim when Neil's about,"
she said, wiping her beak on her flipper as
Pom gobbled down the disgusting morsel.
"But he does love teasing that seal!"

# Animal Antics

"Pom knows all about teasing," said Pepper.

Pom burped. A nasty look crossed his face. He gave Pepper a sly smile. "And I hear that Pepper knows all about flying," he said. "Don't you, Pepper?"

# Chapter Seven

"Whatever do you mean, Pomsicle?"

"I mean, Mumsy, that Pepper has been taking flying lessons!" Pom chortled. "From an albatross! How sad is that?"

Pepper wanted to disappear into the ground.

"Pepper?" said Pepper's dad. "Is this true?"

Pepper was speechless. How did Pom

know? The only penguin she had told was
Petal, out in Silver Cove. She was sure Pom
hadn't been there when she'd been talking
about Alvaro. Petal must have told Pom! How
could she? She had promised not to tell!

"I don't know what Pom's talking about,
Dad," she said in a trembling voice, crossing
her flippers behind her back. "Of course I'm not
having flying lessons…"

"Yes, you are, Pepper," said Pom. "Mumsy,
she's lying."

Aunt Primrose gave a tinkle of laughter. "Oh
Pomsicle," she said, patting Pom on the head.
"You're such a tease! Of course Pepper can't fly!"

"I didn't say she *could* fly," said Pom. "But
she's been *trying* to fly. You've been trying for
some time, haven't you, Pepper? And you still
can't do it. What an idiot."

Pepper couldn't stand the sight of her

cousin for a second longer. "Shut up, Pom!" she shouted. "Just shut up!"

Pom looked delighted at Pepper's reaction.

"Poor tragic Pepper!" he said, grinning. "The potty penguin who wanted to fly! The whole colony's laughing at you, you know. What a stupid fishhead you are."

"Pomsicle!" Aunt Primrose gasped. "*Language!*"

Pepper couldn't look at her father's confused face. She couldn't look at anyone. She fled, stumbling on her stumpy little legs as fast as she could, pushing through the thousands of penguins that jostled around the shore. Everyone was laughing at her. Her Big Secret was now nothing more than a Big Joke.

She was hurrying so fast that she almost bumped into the last penguin in the world that she wanted to see.

# Animal Antics

"Hi, Pepper!" Petal said. "Are you—" She stopped when she saw the look on Pepper's face. "What's the matter?"

"Go away," Pepper sobbed. "You're not my friend any more. How could you have told Pom about my flying lessons? You're horrible and I hope I never see you again!"

"I didn't…" Petal began.

But Pepper wasn't listening. She flung herself forward and tobogganed away at full speed.

Even eating four fish at Silver Cove didn't cheer Pepper up. Wearily she caught a few extra ones. Then she waddled up into the ice fields to see Alvaro, because she couldn't think of anything else to do.

She found the albatross standing on the rock they used for Pepper's flying practice. He was flapping both his wings. It was a mighty sight. Pepper felt a pain in her heart as she watched him.

Alvaro stopped flapping and looked at Pepper. "We've already had our lesson today," he said.

# Animal Antics

Pepper dropped the fish she was carrying and sat down. "I brought you more food," she said. "I'll eat them if you don't want them."

Alvaro tucked his wings away, hopped down from the rock and gobbled up the fish. "I must build up my strength," he said between mouthfuls. "My injured wing is now as good as ever. Albatrosses are never injured for long. The extra fish is just what I need. I have a long journey ahead of me."

"You're going?" Pepper said in horror. "You're leaving me? Now?"

"I can't stay here a moment longer," said Alvaro haughtily. "The ground is no place for an albatross. I can't bear the monotony of it. The sky is calling."

"I wish it would call me," Pepper whispered.

She felt truly terrible. No more best friend.

No more flying lessons. She had nothing but a bully of a cousin and the giggles of the colony to look forward to.

"Cheer up, small penguin," said Alvaro in an unexpectedly kind voice. "Penguins are penguins and albatrosses are albatrosses. It's just the way that it is. You have a good life here, don't you? Plenty of fish. Plenty of friends."

"My best friend told my worst enemy my Big Secret," said Pepper. "That I wanted to fly. Now everyone's laughing at me. It's awful, Alvaro. I don't know what to do."

"Your best friend?" said Alvaro. "Would that be the fat little penguin who watches our lessons sometimes?"

Pepper frowned. "Petal's not fat," she said.

"Well," said Alvaro, stretching his wings again, "whoever that penguin is, it really shouldn't eat so much. Farewell, Pepper. Remember how lucky you are to have met me."

He started galloping down the snow, pumping his legs and heaving his wings. He had to run a long way before the wind gave him any lift. Even with his webbed toes off the snow, he had to flap almost as hard as Pepper did during her lessons. Finally, Alvaro rose into the air, snorting with the effort.

# Animal Antics

*No wonder albatrosses don't land very often*, Pepper thought. *They look totally stupid when they take off again.* She never knew such a grand bird could look so ridiculous.

This thought cheered her up a little. She stood up and started waddling slowly away from the place where her dreams of flying had all gone wrong. As she waddled, she thought about what Alvaro had said about a fat penguin watching them. The only fat penguin she could think of was Pom.

Pepper stopped short, winded by a sudden realization. Pom had been watching her. Which meant Petal hadn't told him her Big Secret at all. Which meant—

"Petal!" Pepper gasped. She started waddling faster. She had to find Petal. She needed to say sorry. Or she might lose her best friend for ever!

# Chapter Eight

Pepper's head was spinning as she waddled
down the slope towards the shore. Pom
had been spying on her. Petal hadn't broken
her promise. She really hoped Petal would
let her apologize, and that they could be
friends again.

She had so much to think about, she didn't
notice Alvaro floating gracefully in the sky over

her head. She didn't notice which way she was going either. She stopped, confused.

Icebergs towered on either side of her. Where was she? She'd lost sight of the sea. Silver Cove was that way. Wasn't it?

Pepper suddenly felt all alone and very small. It was one thing exploring the ice fields when you knew the way home. Getting lost was something completely different. She gazed around at the empty landscape. Anything might be hiding behind these icebergs. Anything.

A bit of ice broke off a nearby iceberg and crashed to the ground, making Pepper jump. She was feeling a bit frightened now. She waddled on, checking to her left and her right. It was much too quiet. The sea would come into view any minute now, she told herself. Any minute…

# Animal Antics

She stopped. In front of her, more than a hundred fat leopard seals were basking in the late afternoon sunshine. Every single one turned and looked at her with their perfectly round, inky-black seal eyes.

# Animal Antics

Pepper turned and started running as fast as her tiny little legs would carry her. It wasn't fast enough. She glanced back over her shoulder. Two seals were giving chase, their fat bodies humping lazily over the ice. They weren't nearly as slow as they looked.

"I saw her first," called one: a grey, hungry-looking creature with a scar on its nose.

"Did not, fatso," said the other, who was plump and brown.

"Who are you calling fat?"

"She's mine!"

"No, mine!"

Pepper went faster, stumbling over the ground. It was starting to slope away from her now. The seals were keeping up with ease.

"Hello, you juicy thing!" called the grey one. "My tummy's over here!"

"There's no escape, little penguin," said the

brown seal. He sounded almost friendly. "Why don't you just stop running? It'll be over quicker that way."

Pepper kept going. Her sides were aching. She flapped her flippers, driving herself forward. It actually helped. It looked like all those exercises for Alvaro hadn't been a complete waste of time.

"Bored now," said the grey seal. "Stop running, penguin. I want my dinner."

# Animal Antics

"She's not your dinner," said the brown seal. "She's *my* dinner."

"I'm no one's dinner!" Pepper shouted in a burst of bravery. "Not today, blubberbrains!"

She flung herself down a sharply sloping sheet of ice ahead of her. Almost at once, she gathered speed. Tucking her flippers into her sides, she pointed her beak straight into the wind. The seals were left far behind as the cold air whooshed over her sleek body.

# Animal Antics

She sneaked a sideways glance as the scenery whizzed past. She could see the sea now, and the icy coastline. She'd never seen it from this angle. She was a lot higher up than she had realized.

# Animal Antics

The toboggan run dipped down more steeply. The air held Pepper against the ice like an invisible wall. It was better than being eaten by seals, but pretty scary at the same time. Where was she, exactly?

It came to her in a blinding flash.

She was on the Silver Cove cliff.

Pepper was brave, but she wasn't mad. The Silver Cove cliff was too high to jump off, even for a penguin with dreams of flying. She would never survive.

"Aieeeee!" Pepper squealed as she zoomed off the edge. She was moving so fast that she was still going up. Up, up, up…

For one single, glorious moment, she was flying. She turned her beak towards the setting sun and felt the wind beneath her flippers. But all too soon, the moment passed and Pepper started to fall.

# Chapter Nine

The view over Silver Cove and beyond to the
Southern Ocean shore was beautiful. The
whiteness of the snow was dazzling in the
sunshine. The deep blue water sparkled like
crystal. The gliding seabirds floated like
snowflakes. Pepper saw the golden glimmer
of fifty-thousand yellow ear patches down in
the Emperor penguin colony, and the back of

a porpoise arching far out to sea. It was completely wonderful. Perhaps she would be OK. Anything felt possible, up here. Anything at all.

She was falling quite fast now. Gulls flew up from the cliff in alarm as Pepper sped past, gamely flapping her flippers.

"Excuse me!" she shouted, trying to keep her body from knocking the seabirds' nests off the cliff side. "Sorry... Excuse me... Sorry..."

She could see a number of penguins gathered at the water's edge in Silver Cove now. Within seconds, she was close enough to recognize Pom and Petal among them. It looked like they were arguing. Pepper suspected they were arguing about her. She felt a rush of fondness for Petal.

"Cooee! Petal! Pom!" Pepper shouted over the wind as it screamed past her ears.

"I'm sorry I thought you told Pom about the flying, Petal! I should have known better. You're the best friend ever!"

Petal's beak fell open at the sight of Pepper falling towards the sea. Even Pom looked shocked to see his cousin hurtling down the Silver Cove cliff to what would most certainly be her death.

# Animal Antics

"And Pom?" Pepper yelled. "Alvaro the albatross thinks you're FAT!"

Petal was shouting something at her now. The wind made it impossible to hear. Pepper tried to beak-read what Petal was saying.

"What are you doing, Pepper?" Petal seemed to be mouthing. "You'll be killed!"

"Don't worry about me!" Pepper shouted back. The sea was tearing towards her like a great blue wall. "I can do this! I've been practising!"

She only had a few seconds left before she hit the water.

*Neck out*, thought Pepper. *Feet up. That's it, Pepper. You just have to glide, really. Not fly at all.*

Neil the seal popped his whiskery face out of the water and grinned up at her. "Dropping in again, I see?" he said. "Very good of you."

"Ah," said Pepper.

It all happened in an instant. One minute, Pepper was looking down into the seal's waiting jaws. The next minute, she had collided with a snow-white feathery back.

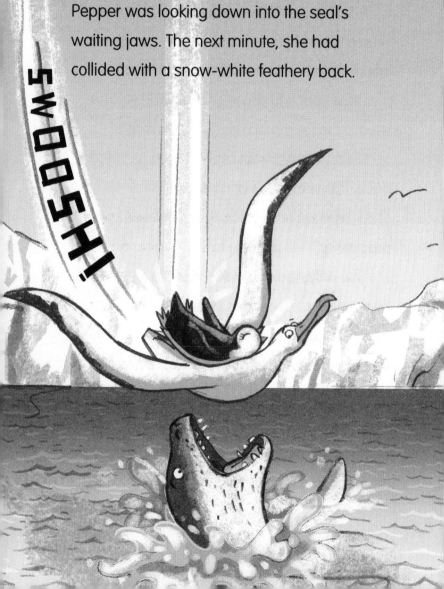

SWOOSH!

# Animal Antics

Alvaro staggered as Pepper thumped on top of him. He had swooped beneath her in the nick of time. "Rather an ambitious jump, Pepper," he said over his shoulder, bringing his wings up a little like the sides of a feathery white box so that Pepper couldn't fall off. "But brave. Unquestionably brave. Worthy of an albatross. Up and away, then."

"Oh DOUBLE poo!" said Neil.

For the first and last time in her life, Pepper found herself going upwards thanks to a pair of wings. The dumbfounded faces of Petal and Pom dropped away from her. She felt like she was falling again, only backwards.

"Hello, Alvaro," Pepper panted. "I nearly did it, you know."

"I know, little penguin," said Alvaro. "I was watching. Now, what do you say to a quick turn about the bay?"

# Animal Antics

Pepper rested on Alvaro's magnificent broad back as the albatross spiralled up into the sky. She lay on her tummy and held out her flippers, balancing perfectly between the albatross's vast wings. If she narrowed her eyes just a bit and ignored the top of Alvaro's head,

WHOOSH!

which lay just beneath her chin, she could imagine that it was her doing all the work.

They were higher than the Silver Cove cliff now. The world was impossibly vast.

"I'm flying!" Pepper shouted joyfully, high in the blueness of the sky. "Flying! FLYING!"

# Chapter Ten

Pepper would remember the next ten minutes for the rest of her life.

Alvaro soared and dipped over the waves. From high on his back, Pepper saw whales swimming deep down in the sea. She saw mountains beyond mountains, more than she had ever imagined. Up here, the edge of the world looked as curved as a limpet shell. There was even something else beyond the horizon of the sea: more land, glimmering in the distance, white and brown and green.

Thousands of goggling penguins watched Alvaro and Pepper fly around the bay. They clustered on the edges of the water, on rocks and cliffs and the tips of icebergs. Several were clapping. One or two lost their balance as they gazed upwards, their feet scrabbling as they slid into the sea.

Alvaro at last flew down over a seal-free stretch of water close to the shore, just as the sun started to slide below the horizon.

"Do you mind if I drop you now?" he asked Pepper over his shoulder. "I really must be off. Goodbye, Pepper. I've had – an interesting time."

"Of course you can drop me," said Pepper

blissfully. "Thanks for teaching me so much and for saving my life, Alvaro. I'll stop trying to fly now. This is all I wanted. Just this. I'm really— Ooh!"

Alvaro had dropped her. *Really* dropped her. Pepper fell the last few feet into the sea with a splutter. She spun about, loving the feel of the water and the way it flowed over her feathers. Climbing out of the sea, she shook the water away from her eyes. Above her the air was changing, flashing with the strange blues and reds and greens that sometimes appear on the Antarctic horizon towards the end of the day.

"Bye, Alvaro!" Pepper shouted, as the albatross glided away, his back stained with the colours of the sky and the fading sun. "And thanks again! I told you I would fly one day, didn't I? I told you!"

# Just a bit left...

*Well*, thought Alvaro as he glided away from the shores of Antarctica. *What a strange little adventure. One of my finest, to be sure. Who would have thought a little penguin would have the guts to leap off a cliff like that? Wait until I tell my dear mate Anthea! I'll just fly around the world a couple of times before heading home. Hope she's not too angry with me for being away for our chick's birthday.*

Alvaro frowned to himself. When exactly *was* their chick's birthday? And for that matter, what on earth was his name?

# And a bit more...

"It wasn't really flying," grumbled Pom, as he waddled back with Petal to where Pepper was celebrating on the shore.

"Yes it was," said Petal. "You're just jealous."

"Jealous?" Pom gave a strangled laugh. "No way!"

Dozens of penguins were clapping Pepper on the back with their flippers. Pom noticed sourly that Pepper's dad was right in the middle, smothering Pepper with fishy kisses. Even his Mumsy was stroking his stupid cousin's head. He hated how Pepper was so popular with everyone. It wasn't fair.

"I'm *well* more brilliant than Pepper, actually," Pom moaned to Petal. "I got away from Neil the seal once!"

# Animal Antics

"Did you?" said Petal.

"Yeah," Pom boasted. "I did."

"Then you'll have no trouble getting away from him again, will you?" Petal said, tobogganing off. "Cos he's right behind you!"

Pom turned.

"My my," said Neil admiringly. "You really are jolly fat."

# THE END

# Totally True

Albatrosses can fly for up to a decade without returning to land.

The span of one albatross wing can measure the same as one average mum.

Antarctica belongs to no one, has no language, no currency and no permanent human population.

Male Emperor penguins balance their eggs on their feet until they hatch.

Seals can sleep underwater and surface for air without even waking up.

If you watch a penguin underwater, they really do fly.

Out now!

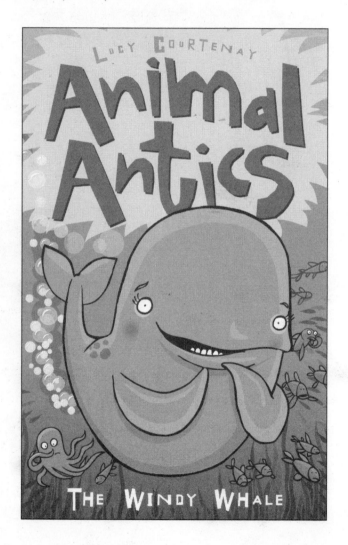